For Jeannie Veltz ~ from your biggest fans, Beth and Osbert
E. C. K.

For Audrey and Flynn ~ don't lend out the family helicopter to penguins ~
or you will be picking dried seaweed snacks out of the seats for weeks.
H. B. L.

First published 2009 by Walker Books Ltd
87 Vauxhall Walk, London SE11 5HJ

2 4 6 8 10 9 7 5 3 1

Text © 2009 Elizabeth Cody Kimmel
Illustrations © 2009 H. B. Lewis

The right of Elizabeth Cody Kimmel and H. B. Lewis to be identified
as author and illustrator respectively of this work has been asserted
by them in accordance with the Copyright, Designs and Patents Act 1988

This book has been typeset in Colwell.

Printed in China

British Library Cataloguing in Publication Data:
a catalogue record for this book is available from the British Library

ISBN 978-1-4063-1851-7

www.walker.co.uk

My Penguin
Osbert in Love

Elizabeth Cody Kimmel

illustrated by
H. B. "Buck" Lewis

WALKER BOOKS
AND SUBSIDIARIES
LONDON • BOSTON • SYDNEY • AUCKLAND

I had just put away my new
helicopter and was cleaning out my ant
farm when I heard a knock at the door.

I thought it might be the postman with my parcel – I had ordered a new wing for the ant farm. So I ran downstairs and opened the door.

Standing there on the doorstep was a very familiar face. It was my penguin, Osbert! Santa gave me Osbert for Christmas last year, and Osbert had been living at the zoo ever since.

Apparently, Osbert had brought along a few friends.

I didn't want Mum to see them (she might not be too happy that Osbert had staged a zoo break; plus, she worries a lot about her carpets), so we crept straight upstairs to my bedroom.

Osbert had an invitation tucked under his wing. When I opened it, all the penguins gathered round and sighed.

ONCE-IN-A-CENTURY SOUTH POLE EXTRAVAGANZA!

Please join us on February 14th for the centennial gathering to witness the southern lights! Be there with your friends as Antarctica's sky explodes in a dazzling display that only Mother Nature can provide.

Yours sincerely,

Aurora Australis

AURORA AUSTRALIS
PRESIDENT
PENGUIN LIFE SOCIETY
SOUTH POLE

BLACK TIE REQUESTED   NO RSVP NECESSARY

As I put the invitation down, twenty-two pairs of penguin eyes were watching me.

Mum was having a party tonight and all my relatives were going to be there. I *had* to go. But Osbert wanted me to help him get to the South Pole. And Osbert was my friend.

We checked the globe. It looked like due south from my house to Antarctica.

Now, everyone knows penguins can't fly...

But I can. This year, Santa gave
me my very own helicopter!

I left a note for Mum:

Mum,
I'm taking the helicopter out for a spin.
Don't worry—I packed my warm red sweater.

    Love,
    Joe

P.S. I won't be late for the party, I promise.

I had a little trouble getting everybody to
put on their seat belts, but we managed
to take off before midday.

We'd been flying south for a really long time when Osbert nudged me with his wing. I picked a quiet-looking spot and landed the helicopter. When we got out, a man in a flowery shirt came over and offered us drinks. Apparently, we had not flown far enough south yet.

It was way past lunchtime, and now the penguins were queuing for the toilet. I didn't know how we would ever get there in time.

But Osbert was my friend. And he wanted me to help him get to the South Pole.

We'd been flying south for a really, *really* long time when Osbert poked me with his beak. I looked down and saw snow-capped mountains. I found a nice flat spot and landed the helicopter. When we got out, a little girl selling T-shirts came over.

Apparently, we had still not flown far enough south.

Everyone was really friendly here. But it was getting dark, and even in my wildest dreams I couldn't imagine how we were going to get there in time.

But Osbert was my friend. And Osbert couldn't fly. So he wanted me to help him get to the South Pole.

We'd been flying south for a really, really, *really* long time when Osbert prodded me with his foot. I looked down. At first I thought we were flying through a giant cloud. But then I realized it was snow — snow everywhere.

The South Pole.

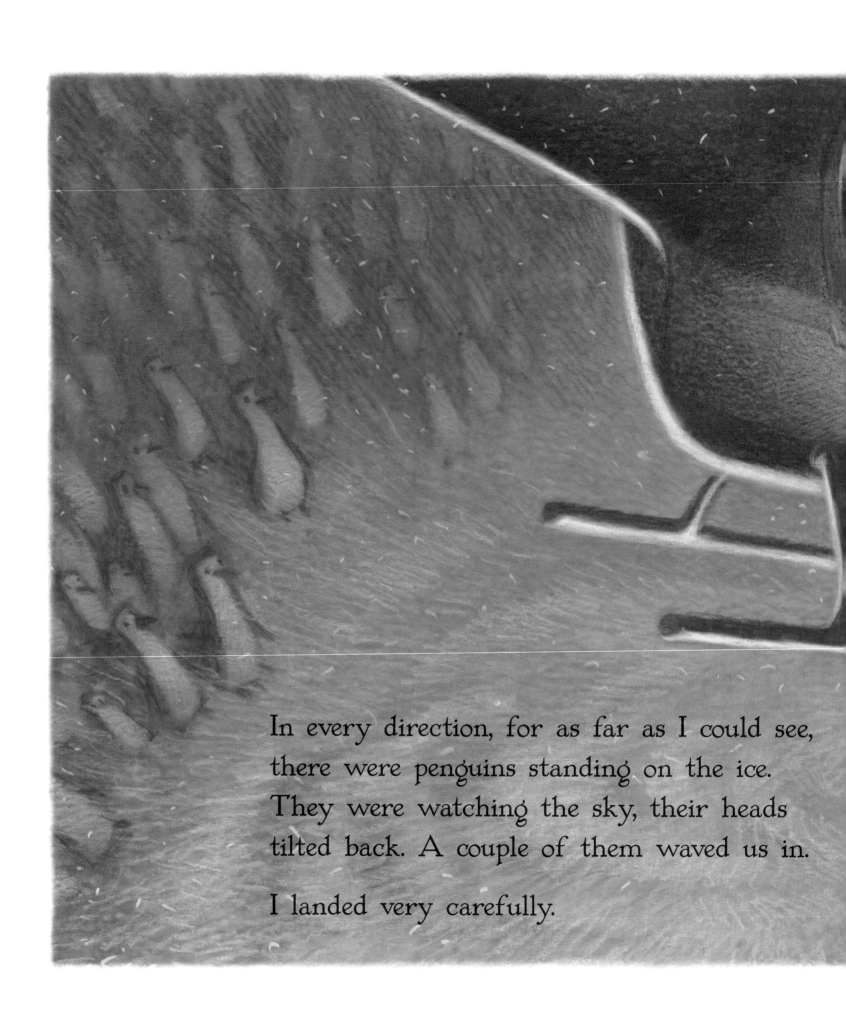

In every direction, for as far as I could see, there were penguins standing on the ice. They were watching the sky, their heads tilted back. A couple of them waved us in.

I landed very carefully.

Fortunately, Osbert and the penguins were already wearing their party clothes. I put a black tie on over my warm red sweater and we all jumped out.

Wow! The southern lights were even better than the invitation had said! There was nothing like this back home. It was way better than any sunset or fireworks show.

But when I turned round to tell Osbert how amazing it was, he wasn't looking at the lights...

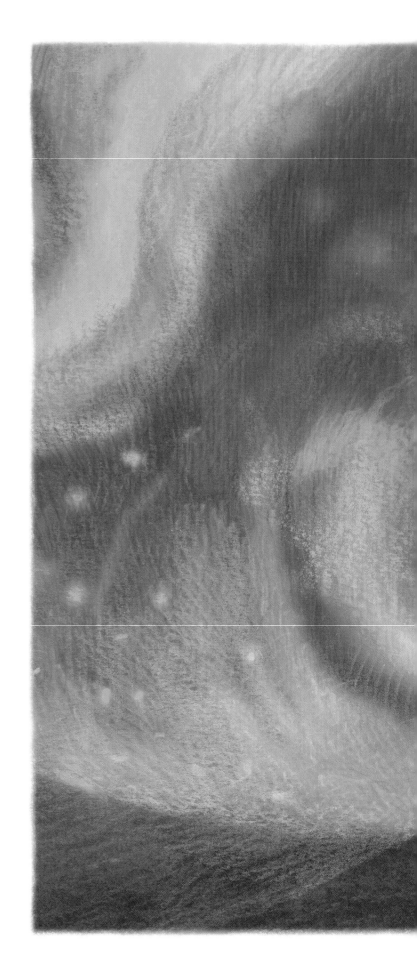

Osbert was staring at a penguin who had waddled out of the crowd. It was Aurora Australis! Osbert's beak dropped open. His eyes widened. He wiggled his flippers and sucked in his stomach.

Osbert was my friend. Osbert couldn't fly. So I had helped Osbert to get here. But now he wasn't even looking at the southern lights. He was looking at Aurora Australis! And she was looking back at him. They were staring into each other's penguin eyes.

Osbert was in love.

My toes were getting cold and my stomach was starting to rumble. I wanted to go home. But before I could say anything, Osbert and Aurora started a game of flipperball.

I waited patiently, and a little icicle started to form on my black tie.

Then Aurora started to bellyslide down an iceberg. Osbert jumped onto his belly to race her. They couldn't decide who had won, so Osbert wanted to do it again.

I reminded Osbert
that I had to be home in
time for Mum's party, but he
gave me the "just a minute" flipper. He
and Aurora started making a giant snow
penguin. Meanwhile, another icicle formed
next to the first one. And my red sweater
had frozen stiff. I knew if I didn't leave
straight away, I'd be late for the party.

As if all this weren't bad enough, I realized I needed to pee. Back on the ice, Osbert and Aurora were making a second snow penguin to keep the first one company. I called to Osbert, but he didn't even hear me, so I went off alone in the dark.

I walked slowly back to the helicopter. It was snowing now, and I couldn't see Osbert anywhere. But I had to go. There was no time for a final goodbye. Anyway, Osbert was Aurora's friend now.

But when I tried to get into the helicopter, there was something blocking my way...

The helicopter was full of penguins —
including Osbert and Aurora! I threw
my arms round Osbert. Aurora patted
my head with her flipper, so I gave her
a hug too. She smelled like seaweed, but
in a nice way.

I asked Osbert if he was absolutely sure
he wanted to come back north with me.
He nodded, and all the other penguins
nodded too.

To be honest, I'm not sure that the penguins in the helicopter were exactly the same ones we'd started out with. But Osbert was definitely the same old Osbert.

And now Osbert and Aurora were *both* my friends. I was going to fly us all home. With any luck, we'd even be back in time for the party.

On the last leg of the trip, I let Osbert take the controls...

It turns out penguins can fly really well after all!

THROW A PARTY
FOR YOUR FRIENDS!

Why not invite your friends over for a penguin party. Using multicoloured pens, paper, glitter and glue, make some eye-catching invitations, telling your friends the date and time and where to come. You could also ask your friends to come in costume – as a penguin, of course! All you need to dress up as Osbert or Aurora is a white T-shirt and a black hooded sweatshirt, shirt or jacket. You could also try to borrow a bow-tie! If you're really stuck, wear a red sweater like Joe.

Osbert's favourite snack is cold creamed herrings and seaweed jam, but your friends might not like that very much! With the help of an adult, try making these special South Pole snacks instead:

Southern Lights Punch

INGREDIENTS (serves 4):

Ice cubes
Cherry cordial
700 ml orange juice
700 ml pineapple juice
Juice of two limes
500 ml cream soda

DIRECTIONS:

Fill four glasses with ice cubes. Pour a small amount of cherry cordial into the bottom of each glass. Mix the orange, pineapple and lime juice together in a jug and divide between the glasses. Finally add the cream soda. Using a cocktail stick, some Sellotape and a small strip of paper, make a flag that says South Pole and then stick it into your ice-cube iceberg.

Black-and-White Penguin Cookies

INGREDIENTS:

225 g unsalted butter
400 g caster sugar
4 eggs
230 ml milk
1 teaspoon vanilla essence
1 tablespoon lemon juice
600 g plain flour
1 teaspoon baking powder
1/2 teaspoon salt
600 g icing sugar
100 ml warm water
100 g dark chocolate, broken into pieces

DIRECTIONS (you will need an adult to help):

1. Preheat oven to 375° F, 190° C, gas mark 5. Grease two baking trays.

2. Mix the butter and sugar in a bowl until smooth. Beat in the eggs, one at a time. Stir in the milk, vanilla essence and lemon juice. In a separate bowl combine the flour, baking powder and salt. Spoon this mixture gradually into the butter and sugar mixture and blend. Use a tablespoon to put dollops of dough onto the baking trays, five centimetres apart.

3. Bake until the edges begin to brown (20–30 minutes). Transfer the cookies to a wire rack and allow to cool completely.

4. To make the icing, put the icing sugar in a large bowl. Mix in the warm water, one tablespoon at a time, until the mixture is thick and spreadable. (Add more water if you need to.) Transfer half the mixture into a second bowl.

5. Half fill a saucepan with water and bring to the boil. Put the chocolate into a bowl and place over the saucepan. Stir the chocolate until it melts, then remove from the heat and allow to cool. Add the melted chocolate to one of bowls of icing.

6. With a pastry brush, coat half of each cookie with chocolate icing and allow to set before coating the other half with white icing.